2020!

Dedicated to the selfless, heroic actions of our frontline workers in combatting a global pandemic. Against an invisible enemy across the globe, you showed relentless courage, personal sacrifice, and tremendous compassion.

Dedicated to our precious seniors around the world and specifically to my amazing 93-year-old parents who I love beyond words. Your "incarceration" was intended to protect you from life-threatening illness, but you faced unexpected isolation, confusion and loneliness while locked down. You showed strength and patience in spite of being unable to share the past year of your lives with beloved family and friends.

Dedicated to every child who continues to sort through uncertainties the pandemic poured into daily life. Your greatest setbacks of 2020 provided lessons for your greatest comebacks in life. Dream big and hold fast to your ideals, and your resilience will awaken the child in all of us.

When life seems out of control like it did in 2020, we often turn to humor to help us gain back control. Humor can sustain us in our darkest days. May the silliness of this book hang out in your home for a little while, and may Shelby Shoes find her way into your heart and leave a smile on your face.

~To my loves Phil, Brady, Jelena, Davor, Liam, Nick, Andrea, Mallory, Scott and baby girl, you are my heart and my world~

Shelby Shoes

and

Piggy's Pandemic Pandemonium

by Sue Ellen Miner

illustrated by Tracey Arvidson

This is Shelby Shoes.

This is her favorite toy, Piggy.

Piggy is missing.
Piggy is missing during a pandemic.

Piggy is in a pickle.

Piggy is in a pandemic pickle.

Shelby Shoes wants to look for Piggy,
but first …

She must have a good plan and get help from her friends. Shelby Shoes has an idea.

She will invite her friends to join a call and plan as a team.

It will be the Piggy Pickle Team.

She will invite Boofus Boss and…

Abby Lou and…

Jingle Cricket and…

Mia Moo and…

Darty Smarty and…

Hoot McToot.

WHAT?

Boofus Boss,

Abby Lou,

Jingle Cricket,

Mia Moo,

Darty Smarty,

and Hoot McToot?

YES!

Shelby Shoes tells the Piggy Pickle Team that Piggy is missing. Piggy is in a pandemic pickle and needs help.

They talk about a Piggy Pickle Team plan to look everywhere to find Piggy,

and get Piggy out of this pandemic pickle.

They plan and plan and ask very good questions, like…

Can Boofus Boss help look for Piggy without wearing his mask?

NO!

Boofus Boss cannot help look for Piggy without wearing his mask. That would surely be so silly.

Can Abby Lou help look for Piggy with two dirty paws?

NO!

Abby Lou cannot help look for Piggy with two dirty paws. That would surely be so silly.

Can Jingle Cricket walk right beside Mia Moo while looking for Piggy?

NO!

Jingle Cricket cannot walk right beside
Mia Moo while looking for Piggy.
That would surely be so silly.

Can Hoot McToot and Darty Smarty help look for Piggy while walking right beside each other, with two dirty paws and not wearing their masks?

No! No!

NO! NO!

NO!

This is pandemic pandemonium!

Hoot McToot and Darty Smarty cannot look
for Piggy while walking right beside each
other, with two dirty paws, and without
wearing their masks! That would surely
be so silly.

Shelby Shoes reminds all her friends that
they are in a pandemic.

They should wear their masks, wash their paws with soap and water, and keep space between themselves and others.

Now, Shelby Shoes and her Piggy Pickle Team have a great plan to find Piggy.

With masks on, clean paws, and safe distance between them, they begin to look for Piggy.

They look under the bed,

behind the potted plant,

and between the sofa cushions, but they do not find Piggy.

Just when they think they might give up looking,
they remember…

YOU are on the Piggy Pickle Team, too.
Can you help them find Piggy?

Piggy is on top of...

the chest of drawers!

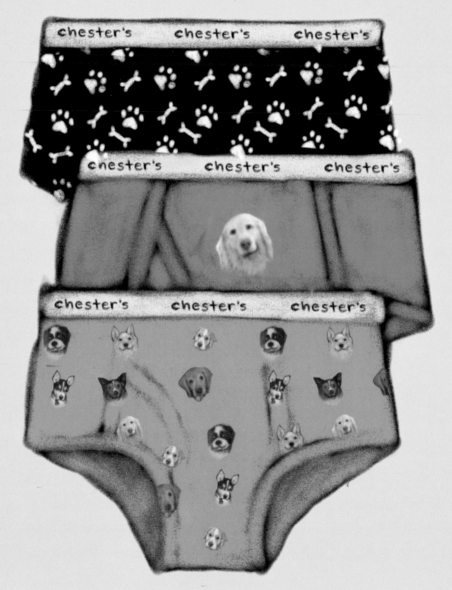

Did you just say Chester's drawers?

NO!

You did not say Chester's drawers.
That would surely be so silly!

Shelby Shoes is very happy that you helped the Piggy Pickle Team find Piggy.

She curls up for her nap and dreams about no more pandemic pandemonium.

Made in the USA
Middletown, DE
23 April 2021